We Are Perfect, That's Right!

Charleston, SC
www.PalmettoPublishing.com

We Are Perfect, That's Right!
Copyright © 2023 by Janna Kay
Illustrated by Scott Simpson

Hardcover ISBN: 979-8-8229-0434-7
Paperback ISBN: 979-8-8229-0435-4

We Are Perfect, That's Right!

A Heartwarming Story about a Younger Brother

and His Relationship with His

Perfectly Different Sister with Special Needs

By Janna Kay
Illustrated by Scott Simpson

To my incredible children,
Madelyn and Riley.

Watching you make this world
a more beautiful place
takes my breath away.
Don't ever stop being you.
You are perfect just the way you are.

Love,
Mommy

You are my sister.
You are my best friend.

We do things a little differently.
But we are perfect. That's right!

You are silly and funny.
When you laugh, I laugh too!

When you jump on the bed,
I'm right there to jump with you!

You love your puppy.
So, I love your puppy too!

Don't forget to bring Puppy!
He will miss you!

Each night we go out and
search for the moon.
You love the moon,
so I love the moon too!

You taught me everything you know.
I look up to you.

I am young and fearless.
You look up to me too!

It does seem a little loud in here.
Yes—maybe you are right!

Let's go, my best friend.
Maybe the moon is out tonight!

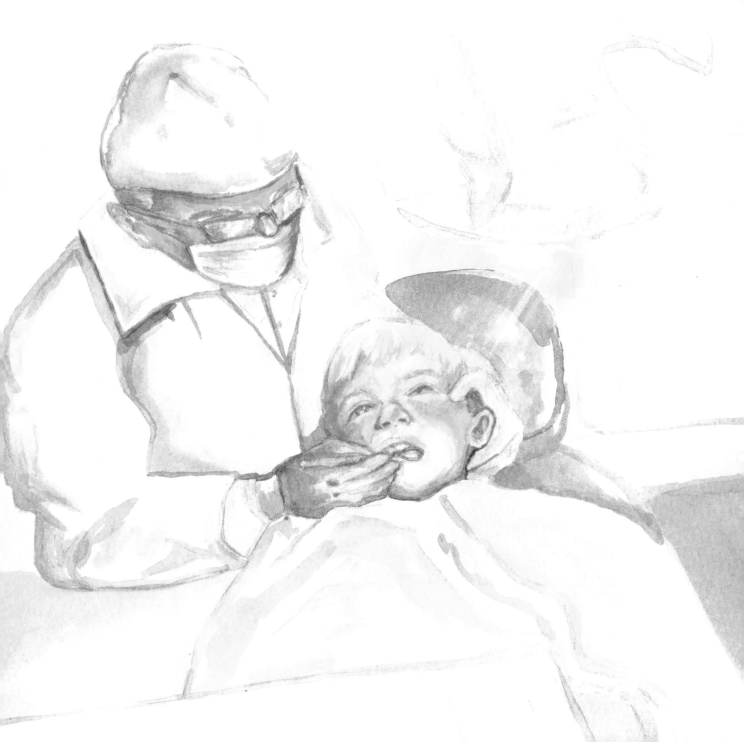

It's time to go to the dentist!
Getting your teeth cleaned can
be scary; it's true.
I'll go first, and then I'll be right
there next to you

We take care of each other, me and you.
If you promise to always be there for me,
I promise to always be there for you.

Madelyn's idiosyncrasies don't get in the way of this beautiful brother-sister relationship. Read on as Madelyn and Riley navigate life and overcome whatever obstacles are in their way together.

Lightning Source UK Ltd.
Milton Keynes UK
UKHW052146270223
417762UK00003B/104